THE DOCTOR,

THE WIFE,

THE MISTRESS,

AND HIS GIRLFRI-END

Based on a true story

BY

GLENDA LEX

Ordering Information: Quantity sales. Special discounts are available on quantity purchases by corporations, associations, and others. Orders by U.S. trade bookstores and wholesalers.

DREAMSTARTERS

www.DreamStartersPublishing.com

Table of Contents

In Memory of Glenda
My mother, who loved
all books!

THIS BOOK BELONGS TO:

Chapter 1

Where It All Began

Once upon a time there was a little girl named Linda. That would be me. When I was in first grade, the teacher asked us to stand up, one by one, and share our biggest dream. Firefighters, police officers, and astronauts filled the room. Then it was my turn. 'I stated I wanted to be a nurse,' and that never changed. My grade school years were uneventful except for this one crazy day in middle school.

There was a boy who had pulled my ponytail one time too many. I had a little bit of a temper, got mad, and pushed him. When I did, he fell into an empty locker. Immediately after pushing him, the class bell rang, and everyone scurried into their classrooms. Later that day I got called down to the Principal's Office. As it turns out, he had found this tyrant of a little boy screaming and hollering to get out of the locker.

Apparently, it had shut on him and, as is my luck, it was the principal who found him and let him out. Don't you worry, I served my time of three days in detention. But I will tell you this, he never bothered me again. It was the only time I had ever gotten into trouble in school which is why I probably still remember it.

Eventually, I graduated high school and could finally begin my journey to fulfill my dream of becoming a nurse. No one in my immediate family had ever gone off to college, so my mom signed me up at our local Community College nursing school program.

My mother, who had married young, never finished school and enrolled to get her GED. I admired her determination and cherished the experience of learning with her, side by side. She often reminded my sisters and I to always have a skill to support ourselves, no matter our husband's occupation.

I never realized how much those words would one day save me. As it turns out, it was just the advice I needed later when I was faced with the task of rebuilding my entire life.

Chapter 2

Off to Work

After graduating nursing school, I got hired at a local hospital in the Cardiology Department. It was such an exciting place to work with the hustling and bustling throughout the hallways. They were doing some of the first heart and lung transplants in the country. Our hospital was part of the teaching hospital connected with the nearby University, and we had young medical students doing rotations through each of the departments.

Jack was one of the medical students assigned to our unit. I had a nursing friend on the floor who expressed an interest in Jack, so I told her she should ask him out. She was old fashioned and said she didn't want to because she believed the man should ask the woman out. I told her that in today's world it does not matter who does the asking. So, she asked him out. Unfortunately, it did not work out for her because the next day at work she told me that their discussion during their date quickly turned to me. I was surprised to hear that but asked her why? She said, "All Jack wanted to do was talk about you," during their date and she figured out he only wanted to go out with her to find more out about me.

The next day Jack asked me out for breakfast. After checking with my friend, I said, "Yes." That breakfast led to more dates and soon we were inseparable. After breakfast that morning we headed back to his apartment where he showed me the photo albums from his college days. It looked absolutely nothing like my college. I saw religious emblems everywhere and a giant cross over what looked to be a stadium. I remember asking him if he went to a religious school. He said, "Are you kidding me?" "Have you never heard of Notre Dame?" I told him I hadn't, and I lived at home and commuted back and forth to the local nursing school.

He was nice and explained all about his college days and the University of Notre Dame. I had never seen anything as beautiful as that campus before and it was amazing to me. I especially remember seeing the photo of the Grotto. It was like a giant cave with candles everywhere and religious statues around it just looked so peaceful there. He promised to take me one day.

The next day I was back at work again. I was assigned a patient scheduled to receive a heart transplant. Jack asked if I could let him know when they were leaving to go procure the heart. I said I would as he placed a little teddy bear on my med cart. It had a T-shirt on him that read "I love you this much" with its arms wide open. It was such a nice gesture, I thought, plus I knew they would often let the medical students ride in the helicopter to go and get an organ.

So, I didn't think it would be a problem. It was late in the evening, and I was working the night shift. Usually, the young nurses had to start on the night shift. Everybody must pay their dues with that terrible shift. I told him that I would wake him up when the helicopter was ready to go. So, Jack went to the back of the hall and slept in one of the empty rooms. I reassured him I would wake him when it was time to go get the heart.

As the night progressed, it got busy. In the morning, when I saw the medical students coming onto the unit, I panicked, realizing I had forgotten all about Jack. I hurried down the hall to wake him up and apologized profusely, expecting him to be furious. Instead, he just smiled and said, "Don't worry about me, I'll catch up to them." Unfortunately, the heart turned out not to be a match, so the transplant was canceled anyway.

That was Jack…calm, confident and seemingly understanding. At the time I thought I was so lucky to have met him.

Chapter 3

The Dating Years

Jack and I dated for a little over two years. When we first started dating, neither of us had much money. We had to be creative on our dates. For instance, one of our dates consisted of going to the Goodwill and buying tennis rackets. We then went to the store for a sleeve of tennis balls. We should have probably just gone out for a jog because we had no idea if we were any good at tennis. Our tennis matches went something like this, one of us would hit the ball and run after it while the other one would hit the ball and run after it again.

We were so happy if we got it to go back and forth over the net just a few times. On other dates we would be going to McDonald's, playing Putt Putt and ending the night with an ice cream cone. Jack would spend many nights hanging out at my house watching TV and eating dinner with my family and me. I would often ask him about his parents, and all he would tell me is that his dad worked in the steel mill and his mom was a stay-at-home mother. He did not have any brothers or sisters and was an only child. He never invited me to his house or to meet his parents. Despite our growing closeness, he remained secretive about his own family.

I would share stories about how I loved roller-skating throughout my entire childhood and even into nursing school. My mother sewed all my skating costumes and since she was an excellent seamstress, I always had the most beautiful skating attire.

In her Station Wagon, she hauled me and many others from our local skating club to competitions all over the country. By the time I was in nursing school I had won over 100 trophies and medals. One day Jack asked if he could go with me to the rink. I said, "Of course! I can teach you to skate." He tied up his skates and off we went for a loop around the rink. He clung onto the guard rail surrounding the area, but it was a disaster. It went like this step, step, boom, step, step, boom. Then, he fell right on his butt. He must have fallen at least 20 times trying to make his way around the rink just once. When he got back to where he started, he sat down and never skated again.

He would get even with me many years later, when he convinced me to go skiing. Now, you would think I would be a decent skier since I was used to roller skating but, you would be wrong. I fell more than I would like to admit and ended up in the ski lodge watching him glide effortlessly down the hill.

Chapter 4

The Engagement

One of the dates we enjoyed going on consisted of heading to our local mall and grabbing dinner in the food court. Then, we would just cruise around the mall gazing into the store windows. But this night would be different. Looking into the jewelry display window, I saw a gorgeous ring that was marked down. He said, "Wow! That's a really pretty ring." It was a ½ carat diamond set with a simple round cut solitaire in a simple gold band. And before I knew it, we were in the store learning about their payment plan.

When Jack said, "Okay we'll take it!" Shocked, I looked at him and asked, "Does this mean were engaged now?" He laughed and said "Yes." The store was Bailey Banks and Biddle, and they had a good reputation in our area for selling beautiful jewelry. I remember the payments being $50 a month. There was no getting down on one knee or planning a special night out to ask me. I think we both knew that would be the next step in our relationship and it just unfolded that way. *If I only knew then what I know now*. We were both excited about our decision and soon word had spread throughout the hospital that we were engaged.

My friends on the nursing floor even threw a bridal shower in my honor. My family liked Jack. My co-workers liked Jack. So, everybody seemed to be genuinely happy for us. There was just one problem. I still had not met his parents at this point.

I mentioned to Jack numerous times how I wouldn't start to plan a wedding without meeting his parents, but he just kept putting it off. So, one day after work I took it upon myself to drive to his parents' apartment. I was so nervous knocking on the door. I had no idea what I was in for, but I knew I had to do it. Standing there shaking, I rang the doorbell. His mother answered and I think I said something like, "Hi! I'm Linda and a friend of Jack's at work. We've been dating a little while and I just thought I would say hello." His mom then invited me inside, and I sat and talked with both his mom and dad for a short while.

They seemed lovely and very nice. I didn't wear my engagement ring because I wanted Jack to introduce me himself in that way. That night I told Jack what I had done. I thought he might be mad at me but surprisingly he was not. I explained to him how I just had to meet them before I could continue our relationship. Unexpectedly, He took me back the next day to visit his parents and told me to wear the ring. I did and they both seemed very happy for the two of us.

One day Jack was visiting my house. It was a beautiful day, and we decided we would walk to the end of the street where there was a local gas station. In that gas station there was a good humor freezer. We would often, after dinner, take a walk and get an ice cream cone and eat it on our way back to my house. But this ice cream trip would be unlike any we'd ever taken before. Jack rarely spoke about his parents but on this day, he told me something I would never forget. And, to this day I remember it so well.

"I'm going to tell you something I've never told anyone before." I felt special. He knew he could trust me and it made us closer. He went on to tell me that a lot of the men at the steel mill where his dad worked would go out together after a long day of working. They would head to the local bar and his dad would often come home late at night screaming and yelling for whatever reason. His mom would lock Jack in his bedroom, if it got to be too late. She knew what she was in for. He would often scream out, "I never wanted any kids and I wish you were never born." Those words still hurt inside to write. No child should have to hear over and over again that one of their parents wished they were never born. His mother, after his dad fell asleep, would let him out and tell him, "Jack,

16

you know he doesn't mean that. He just had one drink too many."

It would be years later after his father had passed away that his mother told me, "If it got to be too late I would run around the second story apartment and put pillows over the vents so the family on the first floor wouldn't call the cops again." She then went on to tell me that he gave up drinking the day our first son was born and never had another drink. I remember him as being a wonderful grandfather to our children.

He would laugh and play with them sit and hold them on his lap and read to them. I think it was his way of getting a second chance being a grandfather. And, he was going to do it differently this time. His mother also told me the last few years of her life with him were wonderful. She was married a very long time, and it broke my heart. She only had a few good years, of him being sober, before he had passed.

Maybe this was the reason Jack didn't have me over to his house before our engagement. His father had recently retired and lost his drinking buddies.

Chapter 5

The Wedding

Both sets of our parents helped us plan the wedding. We decided we would have the reception on a boat nearby. To rent the boat, one needed to confirm a hundred guests. So, we decided we would invite 50 people from each side of our family. Once they found out, family members began baking. Can you guess where we are from? His mom made her Specialty Sandwich Cookies filled with crushed nuts, Russian Torts, Lady Locks, the standard chocolate chip cookies, and all sorts of wedding cookies. You name it; we had it. Our cookie tables went on for miles. Everyone had freezers full of cookies awaiting the big day.

In the meantime, Jack and I would attend church together on the weekends and usually ended up at my soon-to-be mother and fathers-in-law for dinner. Being raised in a

18

Catholic church, Jack wanted to get married in the church he grew up in. It was a big beautiful old Gothic church lined with stained glass windows. Jack was an usher boy for many weddings when he was younger in that same church. We met with the priest to announce our engagement and signed up for marriage classes. At that time, couples had to be engaged for six months and had to have completed the marriage classes before being allowed to be married in the church.

We became friends with the young priest instructing us in our classes. He never forgot us. Every year on our anniversary would send us a card with a note inside it. I would always look forward to getting his card and reading his message. Jack wouldn't usually read his cards, but I would tell him what he said. I remember one card, in particular. The message went something like- *A husband should love and shower his wife with affection so that she overflows and can send the love and affection then down on to their children. And in this way the husband keeps his family strong and protected.* Jack really should have read the Priest's messages.

My wedding dress was white with lace and tule. You could buy the dress with or without the added crystals and pearls. But I loved the one with all the extra pearls and crystals on it. My mother lovingly hand sewed on the extra crystals and beads herself. She even sewed all my bridesmaids' dresses with the coral fabric I had picked out.

Now, I was ready to get married.

The food on the boat was good and our guests danced the night away. After the wedding reception Jack carried me from the boat on to a horse drawn carriage. The carriage was pulled by two of the fanciest white horses I have ever seen. The horses walked us all around the area and over to our hotel. Everyone was clapping and waving to the young married couple as we laughed and waved back to everyone. It truly was a magical day.

Little did I know those vows we spoke to each other on that day only meant something to me. *To love and honor till death do us part in sickness and in health. Forsaking all others.* None of it meant anything to Jack. Looking back now I realize I was just a check mark in Jack's play book. I think it went something like this.

1. Get an education
2. Become a physician
3. Get married
4. Buy a house
5. Have children
6. Continue living your life however you want now that you have someone to take care of the house and keep busy with raising the children.

I didn't know it yet, but my role was simply to keep the home running while he led his double life. This is what I believe Jack wanted all along.

Chapter 6

Hospitals Are Calling

After graduating medical school and getting married, Jack decided to go into Cardiology. This decision required doing an internship. Back then interns didn't make much money, and they worked incredibly long hours. It also meant that it would be even longer before he made a good salary.

Often, interns would just sleep at the hospital. Jack was one of these interns. He would sleep at the hospital and would try to pick up an extra shift here and there while helping in the ER when he could to earn extra money. At the same time, I started working part time in the evenings at the hospital. By this time, Jack and I had three children within a four-year period. Diapers and formula were expensive. Some

22

things never change. All three were in diapers at the same time. I would just buy one box of every size and that usually got us through the week. Both sets of grandparents would take turns coming over to the house and watching them for a few hours in the evenings until Jack would get home. Thank heavens for grandparents is all I'm going to say about that!

Okay, remember how I told you Jack would spend nights at the hospital? Well one day I was on the floor playing with the kids when the phone rang. The voice on the other end was unfamiliar, but his words cut through me like a blade. Do you know where your husband is? he asked. I gripped the receiver. "Yes, he's at work. Why?" There was a pause on the other end. Then he simply said, "Maybe you should check again." He went on to explain that his wife was also doing an internship. He continued saying when he had checked her overnight bag, what he found in there was not what he was expecting.

So, I asked him why he was checking her bag in the first place? He proceeded to tell me he just thought something didn't feel right lately. He also told me the bag was full of her lingerie and sex toys. After making his discovery, he said he did a little investigating and found my husband's phone number coming up frequently on his wife's phone.

He wanted to reach out to me so I would know and to ask my husband to please leave his wife alone. I told him I would talk to Jack when he got home and let him know about our call. As I hung up the phone, I sat there in the middle of the room crying with the children playing around me. *What do I do now?* I thought about what I would say to Jack when he did get home. At this point I didn't even know if these allegations were true or not. But I remember thinking *I have three little children here who need their mom and dad. And, I want to make sure they grew up in a loving home.*

It seemed like hours until Jack got back from the hospital. When he finally walked through the door, he asked me how my day was. I began to cry and said, "Not very good." I told him about the call I had received earlier in the day and asked him if it was true. He denied it and said, "She is just somebody I work with." Then, he told me I should block her husband's number so he couldn't upset me anymore. I asked him to stop whatever he was doing, if he had done something he regretted. He never said he regretted anything; he just kept denying it. I never received any further calls from that man even though I never did block him.

I prayed Jack had learned his lesson. I just kept telling myself that maybe he really was telling me the truth. Even though, in my head, I think I knew what the truth was. You know we all have those moments when you just know. There is something to be said about a woman's intuition.

Chapter 7

The Curse of Valentine's Day

Valentine's Day is a day filled with reminding those around us just how much we love them, whether it be our spouses, our children, our family, or our friends. For Jack and me, however, it is a day that brings much sadness, for many reasons.

For instance, my dear mother passed away from a heart attack on Valentine's Day morning. Yes. This day is one of the saddest days of my life. My dad called and said Mom didn't look good and he called an ambulance to take her to the hospital. She hadn't been sick. She and I had gone out shopping together just the day before. I called Jack to tell him my mother was on her way to the hospital in an ambulance.

To which he replied, "This is the worst timing for me." Those words didn't hit me until much later, but they stuck in my head. *My mother just passed away and the timing of her death wasn't good for you?* I never asked him why he said that, and I never cared. I was so overcome with grief nothing anyone said really resonated with me until much later.

Years later, we lost both my father and my father-in-law. This left me in charge of my mother-in-law who did not drive. She never drove. So, many days I would get our children on the bus to go to school, then drive about a half an hour away to my mother-in-law's apartment. I would then take her to the grocery store, to the bank, and run errands with her. Basically, I was her chauffeur for the day. My father-in-law, before passing, had spent weeks in ICU and rehab.

Each day I would take her to visit him until I had to leave to take care of my own family. I would come back home, get my kids off the bus, then it was snacks, homework, baths, and pack lunches and bookbags for the next day. Only to get back up and do it all over again the following day. I am only mentioning this, not to earn brownie points but rather, to show that my mother-in-law and I had become close over the years. She was a great cook and taught me many of Jack's favorite recipes. They soon became our families' favorite meals because boy were they delicious. Eventually, after my father-in-law passed, my mother-in-law came to stay with us. I would help her get in and out of the bed because her legs had become so swollen. Valentine's Day week became difficult for her to ambulate on her own. So, she had to go to a rehab facility near the house with the intention of gaining strength and going back to her apartment or back to our house after. Unfortunately, she never made it back. She passed away just before Valentine's Day and was put to rest, of course, on Valentines Day.

I present further evidence for hating Valentine's Day. We had a family dog, a little Maltese named Peppy. He was such a good little boy, and he wasn't that old. We came back from church one day and found him gone on our family room carpet. IT WAS VALENTINE'S DAY! By now we were both dreading Valentine's Day.

Now, for the icing on the cake. I was in the library on our family computer. Of course, it had to be Valentine's Day. I wasn't looking for anything suspicious. I just needed to print something. But one wrong click and there it was. A message from Jean. Attached is a photo of her and Jack out for dinner. The email read "I miss you. When are we going to be together like you promised?"

My hands shook as I ran to the garage where Jack was cleaning out his car. "Who is Jean, I demanded." His face went pale. "What are you talking about?" he said as I turned and marched back towards the house. "You know exactly what I am talking about." He ran after me. I sat at the computer, but before I could hit print Jack reached over me

27

and deleted the email. Gone just like that. It was like I had imagined it all. It had been years by now since I had confronted Jack about the call I received from that woman's husband, and I thought he learned his lesson from that. Our children, at this point, were in high school. I couldn't remember everything she said in her email, but I knew one thing - this woman Jean had been seeing my husband. In the email she stated he had been telling her for some time they would be together ultimately, and he would leave his wife for her. You could tell from the picture that she took it when Jack had his head down eating. The letter seemed as though she was pressuring him to spend more time with her, and she was missing him on Valentine's Day. And so, now you see why I call it our Valentine's Day curse.

After confronting Jack in the garage and him deleting the email, I began to search for anyone by the name Jean Pasco. It wasn't hard to learn there was only one woman by that name in our area. and she was about the same age as myself. So, I thought this must be her. I asked my nursing friends if any of them had ever heard of her. One of them had and said she had worked with her before.

They worked at the hospital when they both worked in the ICU. She described her as being thin to medium build with shoulder length dishwater blonde hair, and she was always flirting with the doctors. It did not surprise her that she was also flirting with Jack. My friend had moved on to a different hospital to work before Jack had started at that hospital, but she said she knew of her. I do not know why I even googled her. Would it matter who she was? The real problem was he was lying and cheating on me.

My friend also told me Jean was never married, but she did have a daughter. I wondered if the daughter could have been Jacks. My friend told me no because her daughter was biracial, and both Jack and Jean were white. Jack promised it would never happen again. I told him, "Jack, why don't you buy a sports car like all other men going through a middle age crisis?" I prayed that Jack learned his lesson. But the lesson Jack learned was he needed to hide his tracks better.

Chapter 8

Vacation time

Jack and I were married for over 30 years. And, like all couples, we had our good times too. We enjoyed our yearly family beach vacations. Our children were older now and had graduated college by this point, so Jack said we should take a vacation with just the two of us. I was excited because we had not been on a vacation with just the two of us since our honeymoon. Our three children came one after the other shortly after we were married. We had three children within 4 and a half years. So, we never got much alone time.

Jack suggested a trip to Key West, Florida. Neither of us had ever been there before. I was pretty much fine with anything. I was just happy to be getting away together with just the two of us. We had a nice week. At least I thought we did. We took a seaplane out to the ocean to go snorkeling on the reef. It was so beautiful. He held my hand as we swam around and pointed to the different colorful fish. We went to a museum and saw treasures that were brought out from the deep. We ate at fine dining establishments and took walks on the beach.

We only had one strange moment during the vacation. While we were eating at one of the restaurants, I asked to be excused to use the restroom. However, when I arrived at the restroom it was closed for cleaning, so I returned to the table. I saw Jack texting under the table and when I asked him who he was texting, he said it was a nurse from the hospital. We were all nurses. I told him to tell her we were on vacation and to call his partner. *Looking back it was probably either Jean or Becky. Hindsight's 20/20. Becky who? The Mistress of course. Jean was his girlfriend.*

There were big green lizards running around the island everywhere and chickens running loose. I loved all the big lizards and Jack would laugh saying, "You are so easily entertained." We took a boat out in the evening to watch the fireworks over the ocean. It was the 4th of July, and the fireworks were spectacular.

I remember seeing a family sitting across from us on the boat. It was a husband and his wife with their two grown children and their spouses. They were on a trip together to celebrate their parents' 25th wedding anniversary. They were sitting across from us taking pictures of the happy occasion.

31

Jack pulled me in closer and said, "You know, I really do love you." It felt like a magical moment, and I took a selfie of his arms wrapped around me. In the morning our flight took off and before we knew it, we were back home.

Chapter 9

The Cleaning Lady

Jack and I started out in a small apartment, but it wasn't long before we were able to move into a small townhouse. Two children later and one on the way, we moved into a small family home in the suburbs. After completing his internship Jack accepted a contract to join a Cardiology practice. With the job offer came a contract for more money than either of us had ever seen before. The problem was we still hadn't received any of the money. But we had a contract in hand stating what our salary would be, and we began house hunting in an area closer to the hospital.

Jack found a house in an upscale neighborhood high on a hill. It was a beautiful house, for sure, and I never could have imagined we would ever live in a place that wonderful. I remember as a young girl driving through neighborhoods with my parents and all the houses would be normal sized homes. But there would always be two big houses somewhere in the neighborhood and my dad would say, "Well, we know where the doctor and the lawyer live." That always made me laugh but he was right.

Our neighborhood was full of doctors and people with very good executive jobs. We even had a dentist who lived at the bottom of our street. Jack liked the house because it was on a cul-de-sac and on top of a hill. He said that all important homes were on top of a hill because they look down on the rest of the neighborhood beneath them implying its significance. So, we made an offer on the house and to my surprise it was accepted, and the loan was approved based on the contract we had in hand.

The house had over 25 rooms. There were so many rooms I ran out of names for them. The room with the big aquarium was just called the Fish Room. The room under the great room was used for a big train display, so that room was the Train Room and so on. I needed help taking care of the house, so I hired a cleaning lady a few times a week. We became friends over the years, and while she would start on one floor, I would start cleaning on another and we would meet on the main floor to finish up.

I knew just coming back from vacation she would be there, and it would be our usual cleaning day. Well, I thought it was a usual day. As we were finishing up the cleaning, I went to pay her, but I was a few dollars short. I headed up to our bedroom. I knew Jack always put his wallet on top of his dresser. So, I went upstairs and rummaged through Jack's wallet for a few spare dollars. My fingers brushed against something unexpected. It was a photo with a women smiling. That woman was not me. I walked into the room where Jack was running on the treadmill holding the photo up like evidence in a trial. "Who is she?" Without even blinking Jack said a coworker. Coworkers don't live in your wallet Jack.

I saw the cleaning lady was finishing up on the other side of the room and I showed her the picture and said, "Look what I found in Jack's wallet?" She said, "Do you know who she is?" I said, "No, but I'm sure he does." *Could this be the woman he was texting under the table on vacation?* He just looked at me and said, again, "It's just a coworker." I said, "Jack, all the women you work with are co-workers and nobody carries a picture of their coworker around in their wallet. I don't believe you. You're lying to me." I stormed away and up into our bedroom. On the way I stopped by the kitchen and grabbed a bag of black garbage bags. My cleaning friend said, "Are you okay? Do you want me to stay and help you?" "What can I do?' I said, "I'll be okay" as I was stood there shaking.

She left and said to call her if I needed anything. The problem was I had no idea what I needed, but I knew I had to get out of there. I headed up into our bedroom and started to

35

throw clothes into the garbage bags. I really didn't know what to take or how long I'd even be gone but I knew I wanted out of there. I left with my car filled with a few black garbage bags, not knowing where I would go or what even I was doing. Of course, Jack called me and asked me to come home. He said, "You need to come home where you belong." But this time I didn't. I knew he was lying to me, and I had had enough. I wanted to know the truth and I wasn't coming back until I got it.

That night I sat in a parking lot wondering where I was going. I thought I could go to a hotel somewhere but then, scrolling through the want ads looking for an apartment, I came across an ad for renting a room in someone's house. It was a young couple who were having trouble paying their mortgage and had a spare loft bedroom in their house. They were looking to rent their extra bedroom to help make some extra money. It was month-to-month, and I thought I would go and check it out. It was only 10 minutes from my house, but it was on a road Jack would be driving back and forth every day to get to and from the hospital. Luckily, it sloped down a hill and was situated next to the creek. *Perfect! I thought. He won't see my car here. I can park it down the hill behind the trees.*

When I went to see the young couple, they seemed nice and happy to have someone helping with the bills. I called my sister and told her I left Jack. She asked where I was staying, and I told her I found a place close by, but I didn't have any furniture or even a bed. My sister met me shortly after and we went and bought a rollaway mattress bed.

I also bought a sheet set, a pillow, a card table and two chairs. And, finally, some plastic shelves so I would have somewhere to put my clothes. I carried it all upstairs to the loft and that was my home for the next few months.

Chapter 10

Trial Separation

It was hard to sleep at all. I spent most of my time crying and trying to be quiet. I did not want to disturb the young couple. After I gathered myself together a little bit, I called and made an appointment to talk with a counselor. It was my hope that maybe Jack and I could work through whatever he was going through, and I could get the truth I needed. It did not help that he called every day and begged me to come home.

Some days I just couldn't bring myself to even answer the phone, but when I did it was always the same story. He would just keep saying, "You belong here. Now get home. Things aren't the same without you here." Looking back, I'm sure his life was very different. I did everything around the house and now all that was on his shoulders. I told Jack I wasn't coming back home until he went to counseling with me. He refused and said we didn't need counseling. I decided I would go without him.

At this point I told him I needed a trail separation until I had time to figure all of this out. During the days, I knew he would be at work, so I would go over to the house to get some other things I needed that I forgot to grab when I left in such a rush.

Our youngest was still living at home and I also wanted to see him when he got back from work. I would ask him how his day was and make him dinner. I made sure to leave before Jack got back home. One day when I was in the kitchen cooking, our doorbell rang, and our son answered it. The man at the door gave him a big brown envelope which my son brought into the kitchen. He said, "Mom, I don't know what this is, but I had to sign a paper for it." I told him, "Sometimes they ask you to do that," thinking nothing of it. But when I opened the envelope, which my son had given to me, it was from a divorce attorney stating I was being sued for divorce in family court.

I called Jack immediately and said, "I thought we were doing a trail separation?" He said, "We are." I said, "Well I guess not because they just served our son divorce papers from you to me." He was upset on the phone and told me he had instructed his attorney not to file until he told him to. I said, "Well he did file that, so I guess we are getting a divorce now." Jack said, "No. That's not what I wanted." But at this point I knew he was lying again, and he was still refusing to go to counseling with me. I began to feel like I never knew him. I trusted him throughout our marriage, and he would always say, "You're holding down the home front here while I'm out making the money to keep it all going." I thought we complimented each other well and I didn't mind giving up my nursing career when we were able to afford that. Jack had a favorite saying; Whoever makes the gold makes the rules.

He'd laugh but I now realize it wasn't a joke- it was a warning! *That being, whoever makes the gold makes the rules.* Since I wasn't working anymore what I had to say didn't really matter. He would say it jokingly, but I know now that was his way of getting away with it. Surely those thoughts crossed his mind. Once, we were having a dinner party with the family and one of our children asked Jack for something. His response was, "Yes, they are on my payroll." My cousin's mouth dropped and he asked if he really did just say that? His own children are a part of his payroll? I said, "Yes, he jokes about it, but he doesn't really mean it." He didn't find it amusing.

My cousin is smarter than me. Passing your thoughts off as a joke makes them sometimes more socially acceptable. But listen to what people are saying because if they are saying it, they are believing it. Live and learn. I'm smarter now. LOL. After I left the house Jack would call and text me frequently. After all, we did have over 30 years together and we needed to discuss a lot, so each of us could move on our way. He invited me back to the house on numerous occasions, but I never went. I told him I had nothing to say and that his attorney could reach my attorney at this point. Becky would also call and text me. She wanted to remind me to leave Jack alone. *Are you kidding me? Obviously, you never left my husband alone.*

At this point he still was my husband. Other times she would call just to tell me she thought I was a liar because I told her, "Well, you got rid of me, but you still have one to go because he is still seeing his girlfriend, Jean." She must have asked Jack who of course told her I was lying.

Becky was a thin blonde with dark colored roots and larger breast. She told me Jack had helped train her when she went on to become a nurse practitioner. She worked in the office with him but had known him before that for years, since they worked at the same hospital. She also said Jack had helped her financially and they had been together for a long time. *Now I am thinking, did he pay for her school and her breast implants?*

With Jacks mistress and his girlfriend, they both always knew about me. I had nothing to hide, and I did not know I had all these women keeping an eye on me. I think they thought it was exciting to sneak around and get away with it. You know they say it takes two to tango but with Jack it takes four.

41

Himself, his wife, his mistress, and his girlfriend. Looking back, I should have maybe stayed working to earn some of my own money, but someone had to be home to take care of everything so Jack could focus on building his career, and our children and our parents needed me.

Jack asked me to stay over some nights so we could be together and talk about everything that had happened. But by now I knew it would all just be a bunch of lies and I had enough of that. He said he wanted to remain friends. But I could not bring myself to even be in the same house with him, so I left and went back to my bedroom in the loft. I called my sister, and she told me to hire myself a divorce lawyer. So, I did.

Chapter 11

Packing Up

After contacting my attorney, she told me to go and get what I needed out of the house. So, during the days, I began to go over with boxes and pack up my belongings. I took family photos off the wall. I moved everything into the garage where I used to park my car. Jack said, "I don't care what you take. Just take whatever you think you want or need." Mostly I took things of sentimental value to me like my parents' dining room set.

I didn't want to take any living room furniture we had recently purchased, because I didn't want my son to come home to what looked like an empty house. I took some decorations I had bought off the walls, thinking I might put them up wherever I end up. I took our family photo albums and our Wedding Book. I also took the needlepoint Norman

43

Rockwell my mother made me of a cardiologist, but I forgot to take my first-grade photo. Jack always loved that one and he kept it in his library on the shelf. It was one of those old school photos where the teacher sat on the bleachers in the middle. The students surrounding her boy, girl, boy. All of us smiling with missing teeth. I regretted not taking that photo and would later ask Jack for it but he never would return it to me.

One day Jack called me and told me I could stay at the house for a week or so with our son. He told me he had a lot to think about and was going to Florida for a few days, by himself, to figure things out. He also told our son the same lie. I couldn't bring myself to stay in the house, but I continued to go over during the day to pack my belongings up.

I was collecting our mail and still paying all our bills, like I had always done. Opening our credit card bill, I saw a flight to Hawaii there and a reservation for a resort in Hawaii. When I called the credit card company to confirm the charges, they said they were made by Jack. Looking further I found he had paid for two airline tickets. He was definitely not in Florida by himself but rather had booked a trip with someone to Hawaii.

This is why I believe he was pressured into filing for divorce. He had this trip booked for about a month or so and the time was coming to leave. I sent Jack a message and told him I knew he was not in Florida but rather in Hawaii with someone. He texted back writing, "I just made the biggest mistake of my life. I still love you and I always will. In my heart and in the Lord's eyes you will always be my wife." I stared at the screen, took a deep breath, and texted back, "Jack... you are divorcing me. You made your choice. I made mine. We are done." Then I blocked his number. For the first time in years, I had the last word. "I am no longer your wife," I said. Jack replied please go on and be happy. I never will be."

After I left the house Jack would call and text me frequently. I had to unblock him eventually because we still had the settlement agreement to work through. After all, we did have over 30 years together and we needed to discuss a lot so each of us could move on our way. He invited me back to the house on numerous occasions but I never went.

One day he sent me a text with a photo of our garage door hanging sideways and the back of his Audi with a lot of damage and a shattered back window. He wanted to know who he should call to get it fixed. I guess I wasn't the only one with a lot on my mind. Who doesn't open the garage door before pulling out? I just told him to google garage door repair men. As far as discussing the divorce, I told him I had nothing more to say and his attorney could reach my attorney at this point.

Becky would also call and text me. Becky, I learned, was his mistress and who he went to Hawaii with. She wanted to remind me to leave Jack alone. I initially thought it must be Jean who went to Hawaii with my husband but when I asked Jack he said, "No, it's not who you think?"

Chapter 12

The Calls

While Jack was in Hawaii, I continued to pack up my belongings. I called the moving company but wasn't sure where any of my stuff was going to go. Surely, I couldn't put it in the young couple's house because it was already full of their things. So, I called my girlfriend who just happened to be a real estate agent. Her husband was a contractor, and they bought older properties, renovated them and would use them for rentals.

I told her about my situation and that I didn't want to sign a lease anywhere because I really didn't know what my situation would turn out to be. I also had no idea of what kind of a budget I would have since I was not receiving any support at this time. She told me she and her husband had recently purchased a new rental property, and I could stay there paying month to month as long as I didn't mind them fixing it up during the day, Monday through Friday. It would be a way they could have a little extra income coming in while they were fixing it up and a single-family home would have a lot of room for my belongings. It seemed like a great solution, so I moved from the loft into an older single-family home. They immediately re-carpeted and painted the large bedroom and fixed up the kitchen. The rest of the house would just have the doors shut. But there was a detached garage with nothing in it I could use to house my belongings. Jack would still text and call me with messages that read, "Please just tell me that you're okay." And, "I will always love you."

One day I got a text stating, "I hope you'll be okay with me. I know what Jack and I have been doing isn't right, but I'll be moving into your house and know your son is still there. I hope we can work together to make the transition for your son an easy one." I had no idea who sent me the text at this point, and I never had a name for the picture I found in Jack's wallet. I sent Jack a message and asked him what was going on and he responded telling me, "It's not what you think." But he never would tell me what it was then? I had the movers scheduled but still had some things to pack up, so I went to the house to do one final packing up.

But when I got there Becky had done it for me. She had gotten boxes and threw the remainder of my things in them. Family photo frames were broken in the bottom of the

47

boxes and literally anything she didn't want she just tossed in. So, I went to meet the movers the following day. Upon entering the house there was a woman mopping the great room floor. I went over to ask her who she was, and she took her mop and ran to the back of the great room. I found this to be very strange behavior. Just then, Jack ran down the steps and into the great room yelling, "What are you doing here?"

"I told you I was coming to get my things and I had the movers coming."

"Well, you can't be here now." Then, he pushed me through the hallway out onto the front porch and told me to go around the side into the garage to get my things. He told me I could not come there anymore. I figured the woman mopping my great room floor was definitely the person he was seeing. I thought maybe he had hired a new cleaning lady, but she was obviously not his new cleaning lady. Later, my son told me her name was Becky.

And that was how I learned about Becky. She was wearing a Hawaii sweatshirt, so I figured that must have been who he went to Hawaii with. After a few days passed, I received another message from a different number than before stating that she was ready to move into my house. Apparently, Jack had been telling her for years they would be together in the end and just to be patient with him. This time I asked her who this was anyway. She responded, "This is Jean. You know, Jack's girlfriend." I said, "Well Jean I hate to tell you, but a girl named Becky beat you to it and is already living in my house." Jean became furious with me and said I was lying. I told her, "Well I think you need to ask Jack for yourself because somebody by the name of Becky is living there now." The next day I got another message from Jean stating she was devastated, and Jack had ruined her life. They had worked together for 25 years, and he always told her to be patient with him because once his children were raised, they could be together.

Now that Becky was living in my house now, Jean was furious about it. She told me she was going to go over that night and put her lingerie all over the front yard. She was also going to put her high heeled red leather tall boots in the middle of the front yard and wrap her fishnet stockings around my mailbox.

Apparently, they were his favorites. I couldn't believe she wanted me to go with her to do it. She wanted Becky to see what was left in his front yard in the morning when they left for work. I told Jean, "Please do not do that. We live in a neighborhood with lots of young boys on our street including my youngest son who was still living in the house.

I do not want them to see that in the morning when they leave for school." Jean also told me, "I'm on your side now in this divorce." I wasn't sure what she meant by that, but she told me Jack had spent a lot of money on her over the years for gifts, dinners out, and helping with some of her bills at times. "You should subpoena me." I showed my attorney her message about all the money he spent on her throughout our marriage, and she was asking to be subpoenaed.

My attorney said, "Then that's what we should do because half of all of that money spent should have been yours." When the subpoenas went out to both Jean and Becky Jack's attorney tried to stop it. It went to the judge and when my attorney showed the judge Jean's message asking to be subpoenaed for all the money spent on her, the judge upheld the subpoenas. So, they were mailed out to Becky, living at my house with Jack, and to Jean.

Chapter 13

Tax Time

I have always been the one to take care of bills and saving receipts for taxes when meeting with our tax accountant. So, it came to the time when I needed to file my taxes. I called our friend who had been doing our taxes for our entire 30 years of marriage. She agreed to meet me at the local diner for lunch to discuss my situation and what I needed to do moving forward. I was feeling fine that morning and got in my car and drove to meet her. I remember we were meeting at 12 o'clock for lunch.

I pulled into the parking lot and parked my car. As soon as I turned off the engine, I felt a rush of heat come over me. I opened the door and swung my legs to the side thinking I needed some fresh air. When I stood up sweat started to pour over me. I made my way to the front of the building where there were chairs and a garbage can. I sat next to the trash can feeling nauseated, but I knew my friend was waiting for me inside because she already texted, "I'm here. I'll meet you inside." So, I went inside to meet her. As soon as she saw me, she said, "What is wrong with you?" I told her, "I don't know I was fine a few minutes ago. I'm going to go in the restroom and splash my face with some water and hopefully that will cool me off. I'll be right back." That's the last thing I remember.

The next thing I know, I woke up at 2 PM in the Emergency Room on a gurney. My friend was by my side, so I asked her what happened to me. I knew I had met her at 12 and it was 2 o'clock now. How did I lose two hours of time? She said I didn't come back from the restroom, so she went to check on me and found me lying in a pool of water on the floor. She apologized and told me she called Jack. "It's the only contact I had for you, and he is on his way." Just then the curtain opened and there he stood. I said, "Jack! Please leave I don't want you here." He asked if our friend could stay with me if I did not want him there. She had already done enough by accompanying me to the ER. I asked them both to leave. I then called my sister to tell her what happened and let her know I was going to be admitted for observation.

The next morning, I woke up in the hospital room and the doctor came to visit me. He told me he had some news for me. Then asked, "Do you want the good news or the

52

bad news first?" I told him that I didn't care. *I was just happy that they had some news. I didn't know what had happened to me.*

He said the MRI they did last night showed brain tumors. There were four in total, but he was mostly concerned with the largest one. It was the size of a small pumpkin resting on the main blood supply of my brain. He said, "By the look of them they look benign, but they are still deadly. When they grow, they push on other things and can cause major problems. You are lucky to be alive because the largest one was pushing on the main artery of your brain." If my friend hadn't found me when she did, I may not have survived.

I asked the doctor what my options were, and he said, "You really only have one. If you do nothing they will continue to grow and ultimately kill you so your only option then is to get the largest one out. We can then radiate the smaller ones to hopefully stop them from growing in size." I sat for a while and thought *now what?* The first thing I thought of was our children. I knew I would have to have the surgery, and the doctor told me I would have a 50-50 chance of surviving the surgery without any complications.

I asked him what that meant and he said, "Well you could die on the table or best-case scenario is we will get it out. Because of its location, you will be weak or might even have a stroke on your left side. But getting it out could save your life." I asked him when I needed to have the surgery and he said, "It doesn't have to happen tomorrow, but I wouldn't wait long." I was discharged with a surgical date scheduled and a 24-hour alarm around my neck.

Thinking of my children I knew I had to talk to Jack. He would need to give the news to our children should anything happen to me. I called him to give him the news. He seemed concerned but knowing him now, he was probably secretly wishing I would die so he wouldn't have to split assets with me.

Chapter 14

Christmas

Christmas was coming and it was hard for me. I missed decorating our house and having the room to invite all our family and friends over. And I was worried about my upcoming surgery. My sister suggested we go for a weekend trip to New York to see the Christmas windows and a show. It was just what I needed. Times Square was so pretty with a giant Christmas tree and people ice skating outside. It felt like something out of a Hallmark movie.

After checking into our hotel, I received a text from Jack stating, "Who are you in New York with?" He said he had driven by my rental house and saw a car there that he didn't recognize. It was my sister's new car she had gotten before we left. But I wasn't about to tell him anything more than I had to at this point. I did eventually have to give the court my new address for sending things back and forth and his attorney must have given him my new address. When we checked into the hotel, I wanted to pay with cash, but they said they only took credit cards and the only one I had was the one Jack and I had always used because I hadn't gotten one yet in my name only. That is how he knew I had checked into the hotel.

I paid the payment immediately to the card but not before it posted my location. Again, Jack said that he missed me, and Christmas was hard for him. He rarely asked how I was doing, and it seemed that my absence was noticed more when he had to do anything around the house. He said he had put up a tree for our son. I was glad to hear he had thought of our son.

When we arrived back from New York, there was a Christmas card and gift waiting for me by my back door. It was a sweater Jack bought for me. He would also send Birthday cards throughout our divorce. I guess after being together for over 30 years some things just become routine.

It was December and Christmas was upon us. I was happy to be in a home and have the space to put up a Christmas tree. The problem was I didn't have a Christmas tree. I had taken some decorations when I left and one of the things I took was a box of Christmas ornaments. They were the ones the children made throughout school to bring home, and I would hang them on the tree. Some were Lenox ornaments that had a little bit of value but mostly it was the sentimental value I wanted to keep hold of. I decided it would be the perfect year to buy a real live Christmas tree and so I did. I had the ornaments for the tree, but I didn't have any lights, so I headed out to the store to get some.

My world seemed like it was starting to come together again. I remember being in the store and watching all the families talk about what they wanted for Christmas. The children were bugging their parents, telling them they didn't want to wait for Santa and asking why they couldn't just buy what they wanted.

Husbands and wives were deciding on what they were getting, and the mall was bustling with holiday cheer. There was music playing in every store. I thought it would get me into the holiday spirit more but suddenly, I felt a huge amount of sadness come over me. I went out to my car and sat there and just began to cry. I knew they would all be going home together and I would be heading back to my rental house alone. The sadness was overwhelming, and I couldn't stop crying. I moved my car to the back of the parking lot so no one would see me. I knew I couldn't drive like that. I was crying so hard I could barely see.

After some time, I called my sister and told her I just couldn't stop crying and felt like my life as I had known it was over. I again started to cry. My sister told me to go to the ER, but I eventually gathered myself up enough and made my way home. I didn't sleep that night or the next night and just continued to cry. The third day of not sleeping, I took my sister's advice and headed to the ER. I said, "Please just give me something so I can sleep." They admitted me instead. They did give me something to sleep but I continued to wake up crying.

After a few more days I just couldn't cry anymore, and I felt completely numb. *This is what it must feel like to have a nervous breakdown*. But me? I always thought I was a strong person. I know now it can happen to anyone, and my sister was right in telling me to head to the ER. My sister also called Jack and told him he was a piece of shit. Somehow when she told me that it made me feel a little better. She had never spoken like that and being a nurse herself, I knew she understood what I was going through. So, Jack called the nurses' station at the hospital and asked if he could visit me.

I let him visit because I just needed to see him, thinking maybe it would help me to move on. The staff was so understanding and said they would put us in a room near the nurses' station that had a window in it and if it got to be too much, I could call them with the call bell, and they would take me back to my room. I have worked in Cardiology and long-term nursing most of my career. But my hat goes off to the nurses who work in mental health! They are the true angels.

I didn't say much at all to Jack, I was still so numb, but I remember him saying over and over again how I would get over this. We just don't get along. That couldn't have been further from the truth, and he knew that. We had a beautiful family, and we spent much of our time together laughing. After hearing him say that a few times, I called to go back to my room. He gave no apology for destroying our family. He took no responsibility for his actions. I knew I had to muster up all the mental and physical strength I had to rebuild my life from the ground up. I was discharged in time to get home for Christmas and yes, I hung up my lights and decorated my tree in time for Christmas.

After taking down all the Christmas decorations I invited my girlfriends over for a party to work on our Valentines Day party. I belonged to a lady's group for years and we would always get together to celebrate all holidays. This night we were going to decorate our old school Valentines Day boxes that we would then exchange little cards and candy. The Best decorated box would win a prize. Preparing for my friends to arrive, I got a text from Jack stating that he wished my party would go well and he missed me.

Problem was I had never told him I was having a party. So how could he have known? After my friends left, I began to look through our members and I found a profile with a flower but no photo of them. Her description in introducing herself just stated she was a nurse. I called my friend and asked her who this person was but none of us had known her.

My friend discovered that she had used her credit card to pay her annual dues each year and had been a member for a very long time but never attended anything. Her credit card had her name on it and sure enough it was Becky. She was using it to plan date nights with my husband because she knew when I would be out with my girlfriends. I told my friend and she was deleted from the group for not sharing her photo and never attending anything. Of course, it was Valentines Day.

GLENDA LEX

Chapter 15

Funeral plot

While waiting for my surgery, I had so much on my mind. I could not help but think about what my family would go through if anything should happen to me. I wanted to make the funeral easier for my children. I went to the Catholic cemetery and made an appointment to talk with them about buying a plot. I was told I would have to come back because they had other appointments for that day. They asked me if I knew what section of the cemetery I was thinking about. I told her the section where so many members of the family were already buried.

She explained that's an old part of the cemetery and has been sold out for a long time now. But she would get me a list of available plots and we could see those when I came back. A few days later I returned, and she said, "Well you are not going to believe this, but I think you are going to be happy. You see the priests used to be buried in the middle of each section of the cemetery, so those plots were always saved for them. They just informed me this morning that the priests are now buried with their own families, so I can sell those plots if you are interested but they are family plots. If that's okay, we can go see them."

She took me out to see the location and they were close to my in-laws whom we would always visit for the holidays. I would place a Christmas wreath and decorate their headstones at Christmas, and in the spring, we would plant flowers. In the summer there was always a flag out. Both of our fathers had served in WWII.

My parents were buried in the cemetery where I grew up but that was nowhere near where we raised our family. I grew up Presbyterian but had taken classes and turned Catholic when Jack and I started going to Mass together. So, I decided this section of the cemetery was perfect, and I bought the family plots. I told our oldest son where I bought the plots and I also told Jack. I knew it would be him to have to tell our children should anything happen to me during my surgery, so he needed to be able to tell the children.

Soon after my attorney called and said she had heard from Jack's attorney about me buying a family plot and Jack wanted half of it. "WHAT?" I told her. I don't want to be buried next to him. She said, "Jack's attorney is going to bring it up in court and I just wanted to let you know that before it happened." Jack thought since I used my support money to buy it, somehow, he was entitled to half of it. The judge would not have any of it and said, "Her money is her money and what she buys with it after you have filed for divorce is hers." Thank Heavens because I can't imagine lying next to him for all eternity.

Thankfully, I made it through the surgery. I was cut from ear to ear for my brain surgery. With my head still wrapped in bandages, I remember just staring at the ceiling. The irony wasn't lost on me. Jack had spent years trying to make me doubt myself and now doctors had literally opened my skull to get rid of something toxic. I was healing and for the first time in a long time I felt free.

After being released from the hospital, I had to undergo extensive radiation treatments to freeze the remaining tumors they were unable to reach. My friends would come to visit me, and Jack's partners would stop by. I was always happy to see them because after so many years of Jack working with the same practice, they sort of became like extended family. It was during this time I informed my attorney that I wanted to stop the subpoenas for Becky and Jean.

The date was approaching, and I knew that they would have to answer and appear in court. Jack had created a mess, and I didn't want it to go any further. I knew he had lied to these women for years as well and I knew I was the only person who really knew Jack at this point. I also knew I could put a stop to making the already messy divorce any messier.

During my rehabilitation, I had tons of time to just think about where it all went wrong. How did I miss the signs? I remembered a weird time when Jack was having computer trouble. Jack was having trouble with his computer. He called the geek squad to come to the house to get it fixed. When I answered the door, I recognized the man. He was a parishioner at the church we attended. So, I let him in and escorted him back into the library. I told him I knew nothing about computers but if he needed anything to let me know.

Jack has been having a lot of problems with his computer. After a long while he said there's a few bad viruses on this computer. I can fix them, but I will need to know his passcode. I said, "No problem. I'll call my husband at work and get it." When I called Jack at work to ask him what his computer passcode was, he did not want to give it to me. I said, "Jack the guy from geek squad needs it in order to fix your computer." He told me to give him the phone then, so I did. A little while later I went back into the library to check and see how things were going.

The technician's face was white when he looked at me. I knew, at that moment, he had seen things he wasn't expecting. He said nothing to me, but he didn't need to. He just said, "These after dark sites have lots of bugs and viruses on them. It's going to take me a while to get this fixed." I had

64

no idea what after dark sites meant, so later that evening, when he left, I looked it up. Jack and I never spoke about this again, but I knew these sites weren't something you would want the man sitting next to you at church to know about.

I also remembered how he used to ride his bike on the weekends and would not let me come with him. He would often ride around the neighborhood or go for the day out on the trails.

One particular day he said he was going out to try a new trail and would be home around dinnertime. It was a beautiful day, and I couldn't blame him for wanting to go riding his bike. I asked him if I could go, and he simply said that I couldn't keep up with him. So, I stayed home. He didn't get back until late in the evening that day, but something seemed funny. He came back with clean clothes on, and it looked like he had showered. It struck me as being funny that he would come home clean after a long day of riding. But I knew he always kept a change of clothes in the car in case he had to head to the hospital for an emergency. I asked him about it, and he said he had to swing by the hospital on the way home. He always had an answer. His phone had security on it from the hospital for patient confidentiality, and he always kept it locked.

One day he told me that winter was coming, and there was a new stationary bike he wanted to buy. You could actually travel on any road around the world with the virtual computer screen in real time. You could even talk to other people on the roads as you were going and look at all the sites in real time, as if you were there. He told me the bike was going to be expensive so he just wanted to let me know.

Later, when I began to get suspicious, I Google him and his mistress Becky... just out of curiosity. I wanted to see if anything came up that had the two of them connected. Sure enough, they both had the same bike and had been riding together every evening. I'm guessing we bought two of those bikes, one for him and one for her. No wonder it was so expensive.

I remember knowing something wasn't right. It was hard to sleep that night and many nights after that. One night I got up in the middle of the night and I started to look for his phone. I was thinking maybe something on there would clue me into what was really going on. After searching for quite a while, I found it under the sofa in his library - charging.

Who charges their phone under the sofa? *I know somebody who is trying to hide the truth from people.* Since he had it on lock, I could only see the first few words of a text message. It read, "I waited up tonight for you. I thought you were coming over tonight when you were done at the hospital." Later when I got those calls, I looked back and found it was his girlfriend Jean's number. Apparently, she had an apartment across the street from one of the hospitals he worked at. Becky worked at a different hospital where Jack was on staff, so that is how he kept those two apart. He had a wife at home, a mistress at one hospital and his longtime girlfriend at another.

How did I not catch on sooner?

Chapter 16

Returning home from Rehabilitation

I returned to my new home I bought and was happy to have a place to be able to feel like I was getting a new start in life. I couldn't drive for six months, but my new neighborhood knew I had just returned from the hospital and would offer to drop groceries off for me when they went shopping. I picked a nice neighborhood to move into. Although our houses are smaller here, everyone is hard working and takes pride in keeping their houses nice.

Then it happened again. She texted that she had gone out with Jack, and he still loved her. Others would say he ruined her life. I think she must have been drunk texting because they usually didn't make any sense. One day though she called, and I answered. She wanted to meet me for coffee and for us to confront Becky. She was still furious that she had beaten her to moving into my old house. I told her that I'm trying to rebuild my life and that was between her, Becky and Jack now. She was furious because someone who knew both Becky and her from the hospital had told her that Becky was wearing an engagement ring.

She wanted to put a stop to it because she didn't want to remain a girlfriend again. She had been seeing Jack for over 25 years, she said. That really hit me. I didn't even know she existed or Becky for that matter. I told her we were still in the process of our divorce, and I was surprised he was engaged when we were legally still married. But nothing at this point would surprise me because Jack didn't play by the same rule book as other people.

Every so often, Jack would ask me how I was doing. Our divorce had been going on for some time now, and I figured his attorney was telling him not to settle with me. I think they were both hoping I would pass away so he would not have to split any assets with me. Our divorce took over six years to complete, mostly because Jack was dragging his feet wishing he wouldn't have to settle with me. He was older now and close to retirement and I was getting half of everything. *Guess he never heard the saying it's cheaper to keep her. LOL.*

Chapter 17

House Appraisal

Since our divorce had taken so long, the court asked us to get an updated house appraisal to establish market value. The housing market had changed quite a bit in 6 years. I called the woman who initially appraised the home years earlier and thankfully she was still working at the same firm. We scheduled a date for the appraisal and my attorney sent the date to Jack's attorney.

When we showed up at the house, it wasn't Jack who answered the door but Becky. She said, "I'm not letting any of you into my house until I call Jack." She then slammed the door in our faces. Standing on the front porch the appraiser said, "I guess you need to call your attorney because she's not letting you into your house."

When I called my attorney, she advised me to call the police. Just as I was calling the police, Becky opened the door and handed me the phone. Jack was on the other side on the phone, and I told him "My attorney said I should call the police so that's what I'm going to do." Jack said, "Put Becky on the phone." I handed the phone back to her and again she slammed the door at us, so I started to call the police.

Before I could finish the call, she opened the door and said that we could come in. When we stepped inside, she threw herself backwards and fell onto the bottom of the hallway steps. I decided to stand by the appraiser going through the house. Becky would just keep making remarks. "Look how this is. I would never have picked that color." She was quite annoying throughout the entire appraisal.

When we headed to the lower level, I told the appraiser that there was a bedroom and a wine cellar on that level. When she opened the door, the rooms were filled from bottom to top with furniture and other household items. She could not measure or even get into those rooms.

As we headed towards the exercise room, Jack flew down the steps running towards us. When he got to where we were standing, he was out of breath and just sat on the steps huffing and puffing. When he caught his breath, he said, "Linda, why are you in the house again?" I chose not to answer as he already knew what the appraiser was doing in the house. He turned as white as a ghost, but after a few moments got up and started to go with us around the rest of the house.

The appraiser said, "He has let the house go since the last time I was here. This is commonly done so the appraisal value drops and then you get less from the current home value. After you settle, he will redo what he wants to get the property value back up." That is exactly what Jack did.

Chapter 18

Neighborhood Lunch

My old neighbors would get together for lunch every so often, so they invited me to join them one day. I went because we were all still friends and I thought it would be nice to see them all again. During lunch my one neighbor told me she and a few other ladies in the neighborhood had started to go to a local gym together for yoga. She then told me Becky came in one day carrying her yoga mat and placed it on the floor next to them stating, "I think we are all neighbors?" They, not knowing her asked her where she lived and she told them the big red brick house on the hill.

My friends said, "Oh, Linda's old house." She looked at them and said, "Well, it's my house now." At that point my friends picked up their mats and headed to the opposite side of the room. You have got to love good friends. Becky never was seen at class again.

Chapter 19

Divorce Agreement

After going through divorce for a number of years, the courts finally scheduled a date for everyone to appear. After so long they just want to get it off the books. They schedule both parties and their attorneys an appointment with a judge. If you can't come to an agreement by then, the judge simply adds all the assets together and divides it in half.

They pretty much force people to accept the terms of the judge. I felt half of all our assets was fair, so I agreed to the terms of our divorce agreement. If one doesn't accept the terms, then both parties can proceed to trial.

A trial would mean bringing the subpoenas back up and having Becky and Jean testify in court. I simply just wanted to move on with my life.

Chapter 20

Married Again

After agreeing to the divorce settlement, it was a few days later and, I remember it being late on a Friday night, well past the hours the court would have been open. I believe it was around 10 PM in the evening when I received an email from my attorney stating I needed to provide an E signature on the divorce decree.

I knew the courts closed around 5 o'clock Monday-Thursday and even earlier on Friday's. Even though, I thought it was odd to have such an urgent request. I signed it anyway because I knew it was the next step in completing our divorce, and I was happy to be able to put this part behind me.

Since the courts were closed late Friday and they don't work on weekends, the divorce decree was not put in and dated into effect until the following Monday. Oddly, Jack had gotten married in California on a beach somewhere that previous Saturday morning. So now I know what the urgency was to sign the decree. He was still legally married to me. Regardless, he got married that Saturday, and we were not officially divorced until the following Monday.

I still don't understand the rush with everything, but I'm sure Becky had been engaged for some time now and was anxious to get married. She had a lot to gain. She got a big home in a nice neighborhood and the prestige of being married to a physician.

What she didn't gain was the respect of the neighbors who knew she was a home wrecker. *And yes, I said it. Look up the definition.* These were the women who I would stand with at the bus stop to walk our children back home at the end of the day. The women who would list me as their emergency contact at school for their children in case they got sick and needed to be picked up if their parents were at work. We had become close friends over the years. When I learned of Jack's marriage, I simply sent him a message stating, *"Congratulations! I hope you treat her better than you did me."* To which he replied with a simple Thank you.

I think it was the only thank you I had gotten my entire marriage. Ironically, this got me thinking about how he used to always bring me my tea. I used to think that was sweet.

Chapter 21

Tea Time

Looking back, I wonder if Jack was trying to kill me? I have always loved a good cup of hot tea. Something about it is just so relaxing. All the different flavors are fun to try, and you sip a cup of tea unlike a cup of coffee that you just drink. It makes you slow down and enjoy the experience. It's always been more than just a drink to me, it was a moment to be reminded to appreciate the simple things and enjoy life.

I would often host tea parties at the house and invite my friends. Everyone would bring an appetizer, and we would fill up my fancy tea trays that I would line up down the dining room table. At one tea party we all decorated and made our own tea party hats.

Another time we learned to read the leaves in our teacups. Jack knew I loved tea and during the last year of our marriage he would bring me a hot cup of tea and place it next to me telling me to have a good day as he headed off to work. I was not sure why he started doing that, but I thought it was nice of him to think of me.

But also, during the last year of our marriage, I started to get stomach pains so severe that a few times I had to call 911 to get myself to the ER. I would call Jack who would always meet me in the ER. He would tell the staff that she must have a bad stomach flu, to run some IV fluids, and then he would take me back home. He was on staff there and they never ran any tests. They just took his word for it. He was probably, right? I mean he was a physician after all.

How I wish I would have known to ask for blood work, but that thought never crossed my mind. Jack had a lot to lose. He was getting older and close to retirement. He was looking at losing half of all the assets we had accumulated during our marriage. I will never know for sure, but all I can say is since I left, I have not had any further stomach issues.

So, between surviving brain tumors and those stomach issues, I truly am lucky to be alive. And yes, I still enjoy hosting friends for tea. Just recently I hosted a tea party at my new home in support of brain tumor research.

Chapter 22

The Prediction

None of us know how life will end for any of us. I would like to make a few of my own predictions here.

Becky reads the book and decides she does not really care what Jack does because she is going to continue to live in the house and spend his money. Or she does care, divorces Jack, and takes half of his money again... leaving him broke in his later years of life. Jean, as she has asked before "What do I get in this divorce?" is still seeing Jack and loves him.

So, Jean gets Jack. He is retired now and has lost his prestigious position as a physician. He is living paycheck to paycheck like most Americans because he has lost so many of his assets. So, what does Jean get in the End? Jean is his long-term girlfri-End. She gets Jack in THE END!

Dedication

I would first like to thank my forever boyfriend Mike. Your love and encouragement along the way I will never forget. You have restored in me that good men still exist. And Oh for your technical support as well. LOL

Next- I would like to thank all my dear friends for Lifting me up when I needed it the most. You know who you are but esp. Gail, Terri, Tina, Nancy, Beth, Sindy, Marylynn, Benita, Melissa, Michele A, Mary and Becky, Mary and Helen, Andrea, Heather and Michele S.

And to my sister Terry and cousins Gil and Richard, your words of wisdom were not lost on me.

Finally, to my son John for never leaving my side and visiting me in the hospital or wherever I was. I am so proud of the young man you have become.

I love you all very much!

So where am I now?

I am the happiest I have ever been. I never thought I would say that but it's true. I have a loving boyfriend, that I met by accident. Here is how it happened. My girlfriend invited me to go away for a week with her to her time share. It was another adventurous road trip. One day it was raining so badly that we were stuck inside our room at the resort. We couldn't do anything outside, so we started scrolling around on our IPAD's.

I went onto Facebook to catch up with my friends and I got a notification that I had a message to read from the dating application. In order to read it, I had to create a dating profile. I asked my friend about it, and she had never heard about Facebook dating either, so I was skeptical.

I went ahead anyway and created an account not really spending any time on it because my plan was when it asked for my credit card information at the end, I would just delete it. But, to my surprise, when I got to the end it didn't ask for anything. It did, however, allow me to read a message that was sent from a mutual friend. I read the note, and the guy seemed normal. The next day I called my mutual friend and asked her about him. She was happy to hear who it was, and she spoke about him with high regards and admiration. So, that's how we started to date. I have never been back on that

82

Facebook dating site since. You could say fate brought us together, or you could say Maureen!

I am working again and have made many new friends who are wonderful nurses and coworkers. And to Andrea, Heather and Kristina, thank you for making me laugh and our nights go so smoothly. I made sure to work at a facility Jack is not on staff at. I've had enough drama for one lifetime and enjoy my peace now.

Final thoughts

For what it's worth, I will leave you with a few thoughts. If anyone walks away from you, LET THEM GO because they never valued your presence anyway. If they did value you, they wouldn't have wanted to lose a connection with you in the first place. Everyone has regrets in their life but only you can control your reaction. It is not selfish to put yourself first. Remember what the priest said. You must be full to spill love and affection onto others. Take care of yourself and, like my mother taught me, be able to do something to take care of you, no matter what your spouse does.

I hope my story helped in some small way to offer you encouragement to stay strong and get through the tough times in your own life.

Sincerely.

The Wife

ABOUT GLENDA LEX

Glenda Lex is a passionate storyteller, and a nurse who believes in the power of creativity to connect hearts and preserve memories.

Inspired by life's unexpected moments, her work often explores themes of love, fate and the magic found in everyday experiences.

Glenda began her professional journey in healthcare, graduating from community college as a licensed Practical Nurse before advancing to Saint Margarets School of Nursing, where she completed her Registered Nursing program.

She dedicated several years to working as a Telemetry nurse, providing specialized care to cardiac patients, before deciding to stay home and raise her children.

In addition to her love of storytelling, Glenda enjoys machine embroidery and crafting using her creativity to bring beauty to everyday life. Whether she's designing intricate embroidery pieces or writing she finds joy in the artistic process.

When she's not working on her latest creative project, you can often find her at Walt Disney World, immersing herself in the magic of her favorite place. A devoted Disney fan, she treasures the joy and inspiration the parks bring to her life.

Through writing and art, Glenda continues to celebrate love. Resilience and the power of storytelling.

Made in United States
Cleveland, OH
01 March 2025

14775555R00049